The Feast of the Lanterns

and other magical stories

Compiled by Vic Parker

Miles Kelly

First published in 2012 by Miles Kelly Publishing Ltd
Harding's Barn, Bardfield End Green, Thaxted, Essex, CM6 3PX, UK

Copyright © Miles Kelly Publishing Ltd 2011

2 4 6 8 10 9 7 5 3 1

Publishing Director Belinda Gallagher
Creative Director Jo Cowan
Editorial Director Rosie McGuire
Editor Carly Blake
Senior Designer Joe Jones
Editorial Assistant Lauren White
Production Manager Elizabeth Collins
Reprographics Anthony Cambray, Stephan Davis, Jennifer Hunt

ISBN 978-1-84810-578-2

Printed in China

British Library Cataloguing-in-Publication Data
A catalogue record for this book is available from the British Library

ACKNOWLEDGEMENTS
The publishers would like to thank the following artists who have contributed to this book:
Advocate Art: Alida Massari
The Bright Agency: Marcin Piwowarski (inc. cover), Tom Sperling
Marsela Hajdinjak
All other artwork from the Miles Kelly Artwork Bank

The publishers would like to thank the following sources for the use of their photographs:
Shutterstock: (page decorations) Dragana Francuski Tolimir
Dreamstime: (frames) Gordan

Every effort has been made to acknowledge the source and copyright holder of each picture.
Miles Kelly Publishing apologises for any unintentional errors or omissions.

Made with paper from a sustainable forest

www.mileskelly.net   info@mileskelly.net

www.factsforprojects.com

Contents

The Feast of the Lanterns

From *Tales of Wonder Every Child Should Know*
by Kate Douglas Wiggin and
Nora Archibald Smith

WANG CHIH was only a poor man, but he had a wife and children to love, and they made him so happy that he would not have changed places with the emperor himself.

Onc morning, as he was setting off to work in the fields, his wife sent Han Chung, his son, running after him to ask him to bring home some firewood.

"I shall have to go up into the mountain for it at noon," he said. "Bring me my axe, Han Chung."

Han Chung ran back for his father's axe, and Ho-Seen-Ko, his little sister, came out of the cottage with him.

"Remember it is the Feast of Lanterns tonight, Father," she said. "Don't fall asleep up on the mountain, we want you to come back and light them for us."

She had a lantern in the shape of a fish, painted red and black and yellow, and Han Chung had got a big round one, all bright crimson, to carry in the procession, and, besides that, there were two large lanterns to be hung outside the cottage door as soon at it grew dark.

Wang Chih was not likely to forget the Feast of Lanterns, for the children had talked of nothing else for a month, and he promised to come home as early as he could.

At noon, when his fellow-labourers sat down to rest and eat, Wang Chih took his axe and went up the mountain to find a small tree he might cut down for fuel. He walked a long way, and at last saw one growing at the mouth of a cave. "This will be just the thing," he said to himself. Before striking a blow, he peeped into the cave to see if it were empty.

To his surprise, two old men, with long, white beards, were sitting inside playing chess, as quietly as mice, with their eyes fixed on the chessboard. Wang Chih knew something of chess, and he stepped in and watched them for a few minutes. "As soon as they look up I can ask them if I may chop down a tree," he said to himself. But they did not look up, and by and by Wang Chih got so interested in the game that he put down his axe, and sat on the floor to watch it better.

The two old men sat crosslegged on the ground, and the chessboard rested on a slab, like a stone table, between them. On one corner of the slab lay a heap of small, brown objects which Wang Chih took at first to be date stones, but after a time the chess-players ate one each, and put one in Wang Chih's mouth, and he found it was not a date stone at all. It was a delicious kind of sweetmeat, the like of which

he had never tasted before, and the strangest thing about it was that it took his hunger and thirst away.

He sat there some time
longer, and noticed that as the old men
frowned over the chessboard, their beards grew
longer and longer, until they swept the floor of the

cave, and even found their way out of the door.

"I hope my beard will never grow as quickly," said Wang Chih, as he rose, took up his axe again, and went down the mountain.

To his great shock, he found the fields where he had worked covered with houses, and a town where his own village had been. In vain he looked for his house, his wife, and his children. There were strange faces everywhere, and although when evening came the Feast of Lanterns was being held once more, there was no Ho-Seen-Ko carrying her red and yellow fish, or Han Chung with his flaming red ball.

At last he found a woman, a very, very old woman, who told him that when she was a tiny girl she remembered her grandmother saying how, when she was a tiny girl, a poor young man had been spirited away by the genii of the mountains, on the day of the Feast of Lanterns, leaving his wife and little children with only a few handfuls of rice in the house. "Moreover, it has become a tradition in the procession for two children to be dressed to represent Han Chung and Ho-Seen-Ko, and a woman as their mother carrying the empty rice bowl between them, to remind people to take care of the widow and fatherless," she said.

Poor Wang Chih's heart was heavy and he walked away out of the town. He slept out on the mountain, and early in the morning found his way back to the cave where the two old men were playing chess.

"You must go to the White Hare of the Moon, and ask him for a bottle of the elixir of life. If you drink that you will live forever," said one of them.

"But I don't want to live for ever," objected Wang Chih. "I wish to go back and live in the days when my wife and children were here."

"Ah, well! For that you must mix the elixir of life with some water out of the sky-dragon's mouth."

"And where is the sky-dragon to be found?" enquired Wang Chih.

"In the sky, of course. He lives in a cloud-cave.

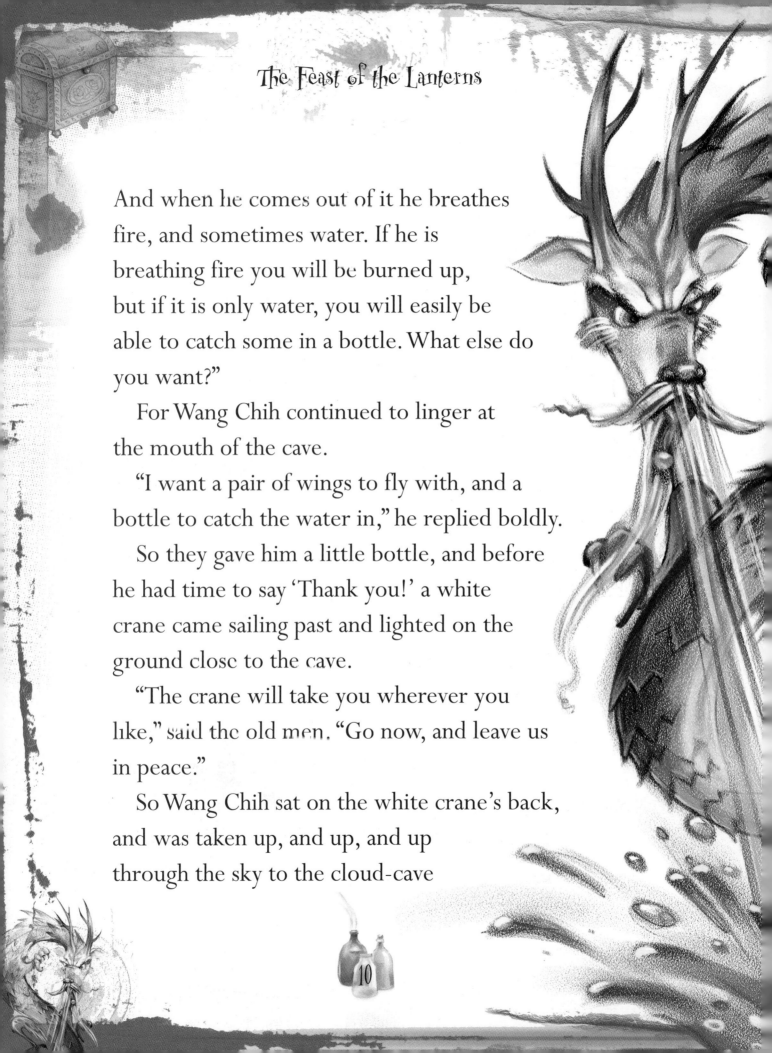

And when he comes out of it he breathes fire, and sometimes water. If he is breathing fire you will be burned up, but if it is only water, you will easily be able to catch some in a bottle. What else do you want?"

For Wang Chih continued to linger at the mouth of the cave.

"I want a pair of wings to fly with, and a bottle to catch the water in," he replied boldly.

So they gave him a little bottle, and before he had time to say 'Thank you!' a white crane came sailing past and lighted on the ground close to the cave.

"The crane will take you wherever you like," said the old men. "Go now, and leave us in peace."

So Wang Chih sat on the white crane's back, and was taken up, and up, and up through the sky to the cloud-cave

where the sky-dragon lived. When he got there, he sat down on the grass near the cave, and considered how to bring the dragon out, and how to make him breathe water instead of fire.

"I have it!" cried Wang Chih at last. He struck a light and set the grass on fire, and it was so dry that the flames spread all around the entrance to the cave, and made such a smoke and crackling that the sky-dragon put his head out to see what was the matter. And the dragon had the head of a camel, the horns of a deer, the eyes of a rabbit, the ears of a cow and the claws of a hawk. Besides this, he had whiskers and a beard, and in his beard was a bright pearl.

"Ho ho!" cried the dragon, when he saw what Wang Chih had done, "I can soon put this to rights."

And he breathed once, and the water came out his nose and

mouth in three mighty rivers.

Wang Chih, who had taken care to fill his bottle when the first stream began to flow, sailed away on the white crane's back to escape being drowned.

The rivers poured over the cloud rock, until there was not a spark of fire left alight, and rushed down through the sky into the sea below.

Meanwhile, Wang Chih was on his way to the moon, and when he got there he went straight to the hut where the hare of the moon lived.

The hare was busy pounding the drugs which make up the elixir of life, but he left his work, and opened the door, and invited Wang Chih to come in. He was not ugly, like the dragon. His fur was quite white and soft and glossy, and he had lovely, gentle brown eyes. As soon as he heard what Wang Chih wanted, he opened two windows at the back of the hut, and told him to look through each of them in turn. "Tell me what you see," said the hare, going back to the table where he was pounding the drugs.

"I can see many houses and people," said Wang Chih, " why, this is the town I was in yesterday, the one which has taken the place of my old village."

"Do you want to go back there?" asked the hare.

Wang Chih shook his head.

"Then close the window. It is the window of the Present. And look through the other, which is the window of the Past."

Wang Chih obeyed, and through this window he saw his own dear little village, and his wife, and Han Chung and Ho-Seen-Ko jumping about her as she hung up the coloured lanterns outside the door.

Wang Chih turned, and looked eagerly at the White Hare. "Let me go to them," he said. "I have water from the sky-dragon's mouth, and—"

"Give it to me," said the White Hare.

He opened the bottle and mixed the contents carefully with a few drops of the elixir of life, which was clear as crystal, and of which each drop shone like a diamond as he poured it in.

"Now, drink this," he said to Wang Chih, "and it will give you the power of living once more in the past, as you desire."

Wang Chih drank every drop of the mixture.

The moment he had done so, the window grew larger, and he saw some steps leading from it down into the village street. Thanking the hare, he rushed through it and ran toward his own house, arriving in time to take the taper from his wife's hand with which she was about to light the red and yellow lanterns that swung over the door.

"What has kept you so long, Father? Where have you been?" asked Han Chung, while little Ho-Seen-Ko wondered why he kissed and embraced them all so eagerly.

But Wang Chih did not tell them his adventures just then, and only when darkness fell, and the Feast of Lanterns began, he took his part in it with a merry heart.

The Storks and the Night Owl

From *Tales of Wonder Every Child Should Know*
by Kate Douglas Wiggin and
Nora Archibald Smith

CHASID, THE CALIPH OF BAGDAD, was comfortably seated upon his sofa one beautiful afternoon. He smoked from a long pipe made of rosewood, sipped now and then a little coffee, which a slave poured out for him, and stroked his beard very contentedly. So it was very plain that the caliph was in a good humour.

Just then, his grand vizier, Manzor, brought in a merchant with a chest which contained very interesting wares: pearls and rings, richly inlaid pistols, goblets and combs. The caliph and his vizier looked at them and purchased some trinkets. As the merchant was about to pack up his chest the caliph noticed a small, strange box. On opening it, he found it was filled with blackish powder and a paper with strange writing upon it, which neither the caliph nor Manzor could read. "I received these things from a trader who found them in the streets of Mecca," explained the merchant. "I know not what they contain. They are at your service for a trifling price, for I can do nothing with them."

The caliph, who was a great collector of old manuscripts for his library, even if he could not read them, purchased the box and writings, and dismissed the merchant. Then, in the hope of finding out what the writings meant, he sent for a man called 'Selim the Wise'.

For a long time Selim examined the writing, before pronouncing the translation: "Oh man, thou who findest this, praise Allah for His great goodness to thee. Whoever snuffs of the powder contained in this box, and says thereupon 'Mutabor', will have the power to change himself into any animal he may choose, and will be able to understand the language of that animal and all others. Should he wish to return to his human form he must bow himself three times to the East, and in the direction of our holy Mecca, and repeat the same word. But beware, when thou art transformed that thou laughest not, otherwise the magic word will disappear completely from thy memory and thou wilt remain a beast."

The caliph was delighted beyond measure. He made Selim vow that he would not disclose the secret to anyone, and dismissed him. Then he commanded the grand vizier to return early next morning, when they would go out into the fields and try out the magic.

Next day, not long after dawn, the caliph and his grand vizier went through the spacious gardens of the caliph to a quiet pond, where they would be alone. When they arrived they saw a stork walking gravely up and down looking for frogs, and now and then clacking something to himself. Far above in the air, another stork hovered.

"I am pretty sure," said the grand vizier, "that these two long-legged fellows are carrying on a fine conversation with each other. What if we should become storks?"

"Well said!" replied the caliph. "But first let us consider, once more, how we are to become men again. True! Three times must we bend toward the East and in the direction of Mecca, and say 'Mutabor', then I am caliph again and thou vizier. But we must take care whatever we do, not to laugh, or we are lost."

While the caliph was thus speaking he saw the other stork hover over their heads and slowly descend towards the earth. He drew the box quickly from his girdle, took a good pinch, offered it to the grand vizier, who also snuffed it, and both cried out "Mutabor!"

At once their legs began to shrivel up, and soon became thin and red. The beautiful yellow slippers of the caliph and of his companion were changed into the strange-shaped feet of the stork, while their arms were changed to wings, and their necks were lengthened out from their shoulders and became a yard long. Their bodies were covered with feathers which were soft, fine and graceful, and finally their beards disappeared, and their faces changed, one after the other.

"You have a very beautiful beak," said the caliph after a long pause of astonishment.

"I thank you most humbly," replied the grand vizier, while he made his obeisance. "And I must say that Your Highness looks even more handsome as a stork than as a caliph. But come, if it pleases you, let us listen to our comrades yonder, and find out whether we really understand the language of the storks."

In the meantime the other stork had reached the ground. He trimmed his feet with his beak, put his feathers in order, and advanced towards his companion. The two new storks hastened to get near them, and to their surprise they heard the following conversation:

"Good morning, Lady Longlegs, already so early in the meadow."

"Thank you, dear Clatterbeak, I have had only a slight breakfast."

"Would you like, perhaps, a piece of a duck or the leg of a frog?"

"Much obliged, but I have no appetite today. I

have come into the meadow for a very different purpose. I am to dance today before some guests of my father's, and I wish to practise here a little quietly by myself."

The young stork immediately jumped about the field with singular motions. The caliph and Manzor looked on with wonder, but as she stood in a picturesque attitude upon one foot, and fluttered her wings gracefully, they could no longer contain themselves – an irresistible laughter burst forth from their beaks, from which they could not recover themselves for a long time.

Suddenly it occurred to the grand vizier that laughter had been specially forbidden them during their transformation. He told his anxiety to the caliph. "Dear me, dear me, it would indeed be a sorrowful joke if I must remain a stork. Pray bethink thyself of the magic word. For the life of me I can't remember it."

"Three times must we bow to the East and to

Mecca, and then say, 'Mu, mu, mu'."

They turned toward the East, and bowed and bowed, so that their beaks almost touched the earth. But alas! The magic word would not come. All recollection of it had vanished, and the poor caliph and vizier remained storks.

They knew not what to do in their great distress. Very mournfully, they wandered about, eating only fruit, for they had no appetite for ducks and frogs. Then they flew upon the roofs of Bagdad to see what passed in the city.

During the first days they observed great mourning in the streets, but on the fourth day, they saw a splendid procession. Drums and fifes sounded, and a man in a scarlet mantle, embroidered with gold, rode a fine steed, surrounded by a brilliant train of attendants.

Half Bagdad leaped to meet him, and all cried: "Hail, Mirza, Lord of Bagdad!" The two storks looked at each other, and the caliph said: "All this

must have been a plot – and we fell for it! This
Mirza is the son of my deadly enemy, the mighty
magician Cachnur, who, in an evil hour, swore
revenge upon me. But still I will not give up hope.
Come with me to the grave of the Prophet. Perhaps
on that holy spot this spell will vanish." And they at
once soared from the roof of the palace and flew
toward Mecca.

They flew until evening began to draw in, then
looked for a place to shelter for the night. Spotting a
ruin in the valley below, they swooped down and
found themselves in what was formerly a castle. The
storks wandered through the crumbling passages
and halls to find a dry spot for themselves. Suddenly
the stork Manzor stopped. "My lord and master," he
whispered softly, "I am sure that something nearby
us sighed and groaned."

The caliph also stood still, and heard very
distinctly a low weeping. Bravely, he hastened
through a dark passageway and into a ruined

chamber. It was dimly lit by a small grated window, and he saw a night owl upon the floor. Big tears rolled from her large round eyes, and with a hoarse voice she sent forth her cries from her curved beak. As soon, however, as she saw the caliph and vizier she gave a loud scream of joy. Gracefully she wiped the tears from her eyes with her brown-spotted wing, and to the great astonishment of both she exclaimed, "Welcome, ye storks! Ye are a good sign of my rescue, for it has been told me that by a stork I shall attain to great happiness."

When the caliph had recovered from his astonishment he related his own story, and the owl told the two storks hers. "My father is King of India. I, his only daughter, am called Lusa. That magician Cachnur, who has enchanted you, has also plunged me into this misery," she explained.

"There must be a secret connection between our fates," pondered the caliph. "But where can I find the key to this riddle?"

The owl replied: "The magician comes once in every month to these ruins. Not far from this chamber is a hall. There he is accustomed to feast with many of his companions. I have often listened there. They tell one another their histories, and what they have been doing since last they met. Perhaps on the next occasion they may talk over your story, and let fall the magic word that you have forgotten."

"Oh, dearest princess," exclaimed the caliph, "tell me when does he come and where is the hall?"

The owl was silent for a moment and then spoke. "I will tell you on one condition."

"Speak out! " cried the caliph. "Command, and whatever it is, I will obey."

"It is this: I also would gladly be free of my enchantment, and this can only happen if one of you offer me his hand in marriage."

The caliph agreed at once. The owl was overjoyed, and she said they could not have come at a better time, for the magicians would most likely meet that very night. She then led them to the hall entrance, advising them to keep quiet. The hall had many pillars, and was richly decorated. In the middle was a round table covered with a feast, and round the table sat eight men. The storks recognised one man as the merchant who had sold them the magic powder! The one who sat next to him asked him to relate his history and what had been done during the last few days. He did so, and among the other things he told the story of his visit to the caliph and grand vizier of Bagdad.

"What kind of a word hast thou given them?" asked the other magician.

"A very hard Latin one – it is 'Mutabor'."

As the storks heard this from their place of concealment they became almost beside themselves for joy. They ran so quickly with their long legs to the door of the ruin that the owl could scarcely follow them. There, the caliph addressed the owl with much emotion.

"Saviour of my life, and the life of my friend, as an eternal thanks for what thou hast done for us, accept me as thy husband," then he turned himself toward the east and towards Mecca. Three times the storks bent their long necks toward the sun, which, by this time, was rising above the distant hills: "Mutabor!" they exclaimed. In a twinkling they were changed, and in the delight of newly restored life, master and servant were laughing and weeping in each other's arms. But who can describe their astonishment as they looked about them?

A beautiful maiden stood before them. She held out her hand to the caliph saying: "Do you no longer recognise your night owl?"

The caliph looked with wonder at her beauty and grace, and said: "It is my greatest happiness that I have been a stork."

The three travelled together to Bagdad, where the caliph's people – who had supposed him dead – were overjoyed to have their beloved lord again. And long and happily the caliph lived with his wife, the princess, with many pleasant hours when the grand vizier visited him in the afternoon. They never tired of talking about their storks' adventure, and when the caliph was more than usually merry he would imitate the grand vizier, and show how he looked when he was a stork. He walked gravely up and down the chamber with slow and solemn steps, made a clacking noise, flapped his arms like wings, and showed how he, to no purpose, bowed himself to the east and called out: "Mu—Mu—Mu." This was always a great delight to the princess and the children, which were afterwards born to her, until they also took delight in calling out to one another: "Mu—Mu—Mu."

The Old Man and the Gift

From *Japanese Fairy Tales* by
Yei Theodora Ozaki

Long ago there lived an old man and his wife who supported themselves by farming a small plot of land. Their life had been happy and peaceful save for one great sorrow – they had no child. They lavished all their affection on their pet dog, Shiro – even giving him more to eat than they had themselves.

ONE DAY THE OLD man heard Shiro barking in the field at the back of the house. He hurried out to see what was the matter with him. Shiro ran to meet him, and, seizing the end of his kimono, dragged him under a large yenoki tree. Here he began to dig as fast as he could, yelping with joy. The old man ran back to the house, fetched his spade and joined Shiro in digging. Imagine his astonishment when he came upon a heap of old and valuable coins. He and his wife were rich!

Now, the old man had a horrible next-door neighbour, and he did not notice that this nasty man was peering in through the bamboo hedge and had seen everything. This neighbour began to think that he, too, would like to find a fortune. So a few days later he sneaked into the old man's house and stole Shiro. He then took his spade and hastened to his own field. As soon as he reached a yenoki tree, he said to Shiro, threateningly: "If there were gold coins under your master's tree, there must also be gold coins under my tree. You must find them for me! Where are they?" And catching hold of Shiro's neck he held the dog's head to the ground, so that Shiro began to scratch and dig in order to free himself from the horrid old man's grasp.

The old man was very pleased, for he at once supposed that some gold coins also lay buried under his tree. He pushed Shiro away and began to dig. Soon there was a foul smell and he came upon a stinking rubbish heap. The old man was disgusted! But this soon gave way to anger. He stormed back on to his neighbour's land and set fire to the yenoki tree under which Shiro had found the coins.

Imagine Shiro's master's horror when he saw that his tree was ablaze! In a panic, he and his wife ran to fetch water to put out the flames. But by the time they quenched the fire, the tree was charred and dead. The old man cut it down and saved an unburned, thick, sturdy branch. He hollowed it out and made a bowl. He thought that his wife could use it for making rice cakes in, to offer to the gods in thanks for their blessings.

No sooner had his wife begun to pound the rice, than it began to grow till it was about five times the original amount, and the cakes were turned out of the bowl as if an invisible hand were at work. The old man and his wife tasted the cakes and found them nicer than any other food. So from then they never troubled about food, they lived upon the cakes with which the bowl never ceased to supply them.

The greedy neighbour, hearing of this new piece of good luck, was filled with envy as before, and called on the old man to borrow the wonderful bowl. The old man was too kind to refuse.

Several days passed and the neighbour did not bring the bowl back, so Shiro's master went to ask for it. He found his neighbour sitting by a fire. The wicked neighbour said haughtily: "Have you come to ask me for your bowl? When I tried to pound cakes in it only some horrid smelling stuff came out. So I broke it into pieces and now I am burning it."

The good old man calmly said: "If you had asked me for the cakes, I would have given you as many as ever you wanted. Now please give me my bowl – even though it is but ashes."

The neighbour grudgingly agreed, and the old man carried home a basket full of ashes. Just as he reached his garden, a gust of wind blew some onto his trees. It was late autumn and all the trees had shed their leaves, but no sooner did the ashes touch their branches than the cherry trees, the plum trees, and all other blossoming shrubs burst into bloom, so that the old man's garden was suddenly transformed into a beautiful picture of spring.

The story of the old man's beautiful garden spread far and wide. It even reached the ears of a

great earl, who had a prized cherry tree which was mysteriously withering and dying. The earl summoned the old man to his palace to see if he could cure the tree. Of course, as soon as the old man scattered some ashes over it, it at once burst into bloom! The earl was so overjoyed that he rewarded Shiro's master with riches. He also gave him the title of Hana-Saka-Jijii, or 'The Old Man who makes the Trees to Blossom', and sent him home with great honour.

The wicked neighbour heard of the good old man's fortune and was filled with jealousy. He gathered together all the ashes which remained in the fireplace

34

from the burning of the wonderful bowl and went to the palace to tell the earl that he could revive dying plants too. The curious earl put him to the test – but the nasty neighbour's ashes did nothing to cure dying plants. In fact, they caused blossoming plants to die! The furious earl ordered the liar to be thrown into prison.

The good old man, however, with the treasure of coins and with all the gold and the silver which the earl had showered on him, became a rich and prosperous man in his old age, and lived a long and happy life, with his good wife and his faithful dog, Shiro.

The Enchanted Waterfall

From *Tales of Wonder Every Child Should Know*
by Kate Douglas Wiggin and
Nora Archibald Smith

ONCE UPON A TIME, there lived a simple young woodcutter. He worked all day on the hillside, or in the forest. But he was still very poor, and could bring home but little money to his old parents. This grieved him sorely, for he was an affectionate and dutiful son.

For himself he had but few wants. His mother, too, was always cheerful and contented. The old father, however, was selfish, and often grumbled at the poor supper of rice, washed down with weak tea. "If we had but a little saké," he would say, "it

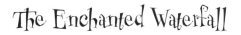

would warm one up, and do one's heart good." And then he would reproach the simple young fellow, telling him that in his younger days he had always been able to afford a nice cup of saké for himself and his friends.

Heavy-hearted, the young man would work harder than ever and think: 'How shall I earn some more money? How shall I get a little saké for my poor father?'

One day as he was at work on the wooded hills, the sound of rushing water caught his ear. He could not remember a waterfall near, so he was surprised when he followed the sound and came upon a beautiful little cascade. The water looked so clear and cool that he stooped down and drank a

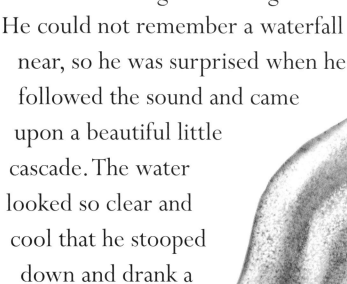

little of it. Instead of water, it was the most excellent saké!

Overjoyed, he quickly filled the gourd which was hanging at his girdle, and hurried home.

His old father was so delighted with the saké that he drank cup after cup. A neighbour happened to drop in, the story was told to him, and a cup of saké offered and drunk with many words of astonishment and gratitude. Soon the news spread through the village, and before night there was hardly a man who had not paid a visit, been told the tale, and smelled the gourd, which, alas, was now empty.

Next morning the young woodcutter set off to work even earlier, this time carrying a larger gourd, for of course the enchanted waterfall was to be visited again.

Imagine his surprise when he came to the spot to find several of his neighbours already there, all armed with buckets, jars, pitchers, anything that would carry saké. Each man had come secretly, believing that he alone had found his way to the magic waterfall.

One bold man took the lead, saying: "Here we are, all bent on the same task. Let us fill our jars and go home. But first let us taste the magic saké." He stooped down and drank, with a face of astonishment which soon gave place to anger. "Water!" he shouted in a rage. "Nothing but cold water! We have been tricked and deceived! Where is that young fellow? Let us duck him in his fine waterfall!"

But the young man had been wise enough to slip behind a big rock when he saw the turn things were taking, and was nowhere to be found.

First one and then another tasted of the stream. It was but too true – no saké, but clear, cold water was there. Crestfallen and out of temper, the covetous band returned to their homes.

When they were fairly gone the good young woodcutter crept from his hiding-place. Could this be true? he thought. Was it all a dream? He drank — and sure enough, there was the same fine-flavoured saké he had tasted yesterday.

And so it remained. To the good, dutiful son the cascade flowed with the finest saké, while to all others it yielded only cold water.

The emperor, hearing this wonderful story, sent for the good young woodcutter, rewarded him for his kindness to his father, and even changed the name of the year in his honour as an encouragement to children in all future times to honour and obey their parents.